Pat is a little
sea otter.

She likes turning up her toes
and floating in the sea.

Pat also likes asking questions.

But what happens when
no one knows the answers . . . ?

MARSHGATE PRIMARY SCHOOL
157 QUEENS ROAD
RICHMOND
SURREY
TW10 6HY
020 8332 6219

Also by Jill Tomlinson

The Aardvark Who Wasn't Sure
The Cat Who Wanted to Go Home
The Gorilla Who Wanted to Grow Up
The Hen Who Wouldn't Give Up
The Owl Who Was Afraid of the Dark
The Penguin Who Wanted to Find Out

The Otter Who Wanted to Know

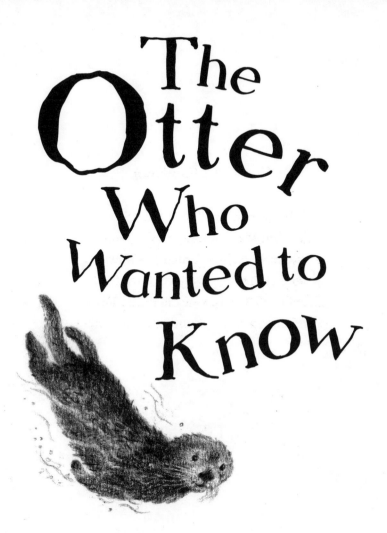

JILL TOMLINSON

Pictures by Paul Howard

EGMONT

To D. H. and all who make life possible

First published in Great Britain 1979
by Methuen Children's Books Ltd

Published in this edition 2004 by Egmont Books Limited
239 Kensington High Street, London W8 6SA

Text copyright © The Estate of Jill Tomlinson
Cover and illustrations copyright © 2004 Paul Howard

The moral rights of the author and illustrator have been asserted

ISBN 978 1 4052 1082 9

9 10 8

A CIP catalogue record for this title is available from the British Library

Printed and bound in Great Britain by the CPI Group

This paperback is sold subject to the condition that it shall not, by way of trade or otherwise, be lent, resold, hired out, or otherwise circulated without the publisher's prior consent in any form of binding or cover other than that in which it is published and without a similar condition including this condition being imposed on the subsequent purchaser.

Contents

Questions, questions, questions

Pat was a young sea otter. She was rolling
over and over in the sea, washing her fur.
She gave it a final wash. Then she lay on her
back, turned up her toes and the tip of her
broad tail, and floated on the sea for a rest.

Bobby was a sea otter too. He had just
noticed Pat for the first time. Although she
was small she seemed to know how to look

after herself. He went over to her.

'Hello,' he said. 'What are you doing?'

Pat kept her eyes shut. 'Nothing,' she said. She knew better than to talk to strange otters.

Bobby paddled round beside her, and lay on the water too.

'Good,' he said. 'I've got nothing to do either, so I'll do it with you.'

'The sea's quite big,' said Pat. 'There's plenty of room for both of us.'

'Yes, it is big,' Bobby said. But he wasn't going to be put off as easily as that. 'It's called the Pacific, you know.'

'I didn't know that,' Pat said, interested at once. 'Why?'

'You'll have to ask Gaffer about that,' Bobby said. 'He knows about everything.'

'I don't know Gaffer,' said Pat.

'You wouldn't,' Bobby said. 'You've kept with your mother all the time because you were only a baby. Gaffer is one of the old otters who lives over there, where all the males live. Now that my mother has a new baby, I go with them most of the time. I like Gaffer best. He knows so many stories.'

'Can he really answer questions?' asked Pat. 'My mother says I ask too many. She hardly ever answers me.'

'Well, ask me,' said Bobby, 'and if I know the answers I'll tell you. If I don't I'll ask Gaffer.' He didn't know what he was in for: Pat *never* stopped asking questions.

'It's just that I don't know much yet,' said Pat, 'and I *want* to know. And first I want to know your name.'

'It's Bobby,' he said, 'and I know yours

is Pat. And that's my mother coming. She's called Carrie.'

A large otter swam towards them. She had a baby otter clinging to her.

'Hello,' Bobby called to her. 'I've found a new friend. She's Pat, and she wants to know.'

'What does she want to know?' asked Carrie.

'Everything,' said Bobby.

'Well, if she wants to know where her mother is,' said Carrie cheerfully, 'she's asleep in that kelp patch over there.'

Her shiny body slid through the water. She had gone to join the mother otters in the kelp patch.

'What is kelp?' Pat asked. 'I know we wrap it round ourselves at night, so that we don't float away. But what is it?'

'I know that one,' said Bobby. 'Kelp is seaweed – very long stringy seaweed.'

'What makes seaweed?' asked Pat. But before Bobby could answer, she said, 'I'm hungry.' Her mother said that she was always asking questions or eating.

'I'm hungry too,' said Bobby. 'Would you like to come for a dive with me to look for food? I know a jolly good place.'

'I always have to tell my mother where I'm going,' Pat said. 'Let's go over to her, and then we'll go for a dive.'

They paddled with their strong feet through the water to the kelp patch.

'I can guess,' said Pat's mother as soon as they were near. 'You want to go off to look for food. Go on, then. I'm tired, so I'm glad you've got Bobby to take you.'

So off they went. They swam round some rocks and came to an inlet where the water was shallow. They dived down, and Pat soon found some sea urchins and sea cucumber. Then she saw that Bobby was hitting a rock with a pebble. What could he be doing? She couldn't ask him underwater, so she rose to the surface.

While she waited for him she took the pebble which she always kept under her arm, put it against herself and began breaking a sea urchin on it. Then Bobby rose to the surface and joined her.

'What have you got?' Pat asked.

'Something special for you,' he said. 'Look. Rock oysters.' He held a big pebble against himself, and began bashing away on it really hard. As she lay on her back in the water Pat spread out her catch on her chest and tummy, and had finished eating them before he'd broken the oyster open.

'Taste this,' Bobby said.

It was lovely. Pat had never had one before. She held it in her paws and licked and licked until she had finished, then rolled over and over in the water to make sure her fur was clean. By then Bobby had opened his oyster and was eating it.

When he had finished he too rolled over and over to get himself clean, and then floated beside her on the water.

'I can manage mussels,' Pat said, 'but I don't think I could open those oysters.'

'There may not be any oysters left to open soon,' said Bobby.

'Why shouldn't there be any left?' asked Pat.

'Because there are so many of us,' said Bobby, 'that it's getting harder and harder to find food.'

'No one else seems to have found this place,' Pat said. 'Let's go and hunt for some more, and this time I'll see if I can break one myself.'

They dived among the rocks. They looked and looked, and felt with their paws. Finally they each found one rock oyster. They had to come up to the surface of the water to breathe again.

Bobby handed Pat his pebble. 'Yours is too small for you now,' he said, 'and I've grown and need a bigger one. I'll dive down and find one.'

While he was gone Pat started to hit her oyster against her new pebble. She didn't want to wait for Bobby to break it for her. It was hard work, but by the time Bobby came to the surface again she had managed it. Soon they were eating together. Afterwards they rolled over and over in the water, as they always did, to wash their coats. Then they floated on their backs on the water.

'Why,' asked Pat, 'why do we have to do this every time we eat? Fur is an awful nuisance, isn't it!'

'It isn't, you know,' Bobby said. 'It keeps us warm and helps us to float. The air in it keeps our skins dry. But it must be kept clean. If it gets dirty we get cold, and then we would sink.'

'Oh,' said Pat. For once she had no questions to ask, because she felt tired after so much diving and breaking of oysters.

Soon they were with their mothers, with kelp wrapped round them. Each mother with a baby had one long piece wrapped round them both, so that the baby wouldn't fall off. Bobby and Pat lay with their paws over their eyes, as they had been taught. Pat wondered about this.

'I want to know . . .' she said, but she got no further. She was fast asleep.

Playing 'dead'

The first thing Pat heard next morning was Bobby calling, 'Wake up, wake up. Breakfast!' Then he put a crab on her.

'Aa-oo-ow!' she yelled. 'My breakfast is tangled in my whiskers.'

Bobby killed the crab with his pebble, and loosened Pat's stiff whiskers from its claw.

'I should eat this straight away,' he said. 'It's lovely.'

So Pat did, and enjoyed her breakfast.

'Have you got one?' she asked Bobby when she had finished.

Bobby didn't reply. He was looking at the sky.

'I don't like the look of that,' he said. 'Those are storm clouds and the sea is getting choppy. We must get farther out to sea.'

'Why?' asked Pat.

'Because the waves will smash us against the rocks!'

'I can't see any waves,' said Pat. 'I'm going back to that place we found yesterday. I fancy another rock oyster.'

'No, you mustn't,' said Bobby. 'That's just where the waves will begin!'

But he was too late. Pat wasn't listening. She had gone round to the inlet and was under the water hunting for oysters. She found one. But when she came up with it she couldn't lie still to smash it, because the waves were breaking over the rocks. They nearly threw her on to a sharp edge.

When she tried to swim out to sea, the waves kept pushing her back again. Bobby came up as she was struggling to pull her slippery body on to a rock.

'Come on,' he said. 'Get on my back and paddle as hard as you can. And close your eyes as we go through the waves. This is your own fault. I told you that we ought to go out to sea. The waves are always worse near the rocks.'

When they were well away from the rocks he said, 'Slide off now and open your eyes, but keep paddling. Now that was a crazy thing to do. Never go near the rocks in a storm.'

'But I wanted an oyster – Oh, I've lost it . . .'

'Well, it was better to lose an oyster than a silly little sea otter. Either you don't ask the right questions or you *never* listen to the answers. I wonder which? You don't seem to know much about the sea. Do you know about whales?'

'No,' said Pat.

'Well, you ought to,' Bobby said. 'They eat otters – or at least killer whales do; but it's quite easy to get away from them because they won't eat anything that's dead. So we have to pretend to be dead, that's all. When you see a big fin coming after you, curl up in a little ball and keep still. The whale will think you're dead, and leave you alone. Come on – we'll practise before we go out into deep water, where there may be killer whales. I'll be a killer whale and chase you. A long way away I'll stick my paw up like a fin. Ready? Off you go.'

Pat swam swiftly away, paddling on her back. She saw Bobby's paw go up. She dived, went sideways, came up curled up in a ball and kept very, very still. She was rather surprised when someone poked her.

'Pat,' that someone said. It was her mother. 'Come on, we've got to go out to sea. Pat! What are you doing?'

'Go away,' Pat said. 'I'm dead.'

'Dead otters don't talk,' said Bobby, swimming up to them. 'I was just giving Pat a lesson about killer whales.'

'A very good lesson by the look of it,' Pat's mother said. 'I have never seen her quiet for so long before. But do wake her up now so that we can go out to sea.'

'Pat,' Bobby said.

Pat opened one eye. 'Am I still dead?' she asked.

'No, and we're off out to sea. Oh, here's Mother!'

Carrie came towards them, with the baby on her chest. They all paddled out to sea together.

'How do we feed here?' asked Pat, when they were far from the rocky coast. 'The water's very deep. We'll never get to the bottom.'

'We catch fish and perhaps some octopuses,' said her mother. 'Bobby, take Pat diving and see if you can find some food.'

Down they went. They each found a fish and ate it.

'What next?' asked Pat. 'I'm still hungry.'

'We'll dive a bit deeper,' said Bobby, 'and try to find squid or octopus.'

'What's an octopus?' asked Pat.

'They have lots of wriggly legs,' Bobby said. 'I'll show you.'

Soon they had each caught a small octopus.

'Oh, it tickles my chest,' said Pat, 'it wriggles so!'

Bobby showed her how to kill the octopus with her pebble, and then they both ate hungrily.

'Mmm,' said Pat. 'It's good. I like going out to sea.'

They swam back to where their mothers were rocking in the swell of the stormy waves. Bobby held out his paws to Carrie. 'Give me my baby sister,' he said, 'while you both go and get some food.'

Pat watched Bobby's mother hand over his baby sister. She clung to his chest with her little paws.

'You'd better stay near me,' Bobby said. 'It's so bumpy in this storm she might fall off. Then you could help me.'

So Pat kept close to him.

The two mother otters went fishing, and when they had had enough to eat they lay on their backs and looked over at their baby-sitters. They could see that they were arguing.

Pat paddled over to her mother as fast as she could go. 'Bobby won't let me hold the baby,' she said. 'Why can't I?'

'Of course you can, but not in this storm,' her mother said. 'The sea is much too rough. Wait till it's calm. Oh dear, listen to the baby. She wants her supper.' The baby was mewing loudly, so Carrie hurried over, and took her from Bobby. In a moment she was sucking away at her mother's milk.

'No wonder she weighs a ton,' Bobby said. He turned to Pat. 'Come on, suppertime.'

'What's for supper?' asked Pat.

'Fish,' said Bobby. They caught and ate

two fish each, before they all went back to the kelp patch. The storm had completely died away, but it had been an exhausting day. Pat was very tired but not too tired to ask questions.

'What makes storms?' she asked sleepily.

Bobby tried to think of an answer, but he saw that Pat had put her paws over her eyes and gone to sleep. So he did the same.

Sharks!

When they woke in the morning the sea was like glass and the sun was already beginning to shine. Bobby had brought Pat some breakfast again and she enjoyed it. But when she had finished and washed her fur she said 'Don't bring me any tomorrow. Take me down with you to show me how to bash things.'

Bobby laughed. 'Well,' he said, 'you've got to learn I suppose. Yes, all right, I will do that. But we'll just lie and talk for a minute now. What do you want to ask me?'

'I want to ask you about sharks.'

'There's no time. Quick. On your tummy. Follow me. No, come beside me.'

'Why?' Pat said.

'Save your breath and come as fast as you can to the beach, and then we're going to climb on to the beach. There are sharks behind us. Don't look. Just keep moving. Fast.'

So Pat did. They scrambled on to the sand and lolloped up the beach. They had their stones tucked under one arm, so they had to move on just one paw and their two fin-like feet. They were very clumsy, but they could move quite fast.

'Now,' said Bobby. 'Turn round and look.'

Pat did. There were fins sticking up in the

water, and they could see tails lashing about.

'Well, I didn't mean you to learn about sharks quite like that. They can swim faster than us but they can't come on land, so, if you see a shark coming near you the best thing is to get to a beach or on rocks, as quickly as you can.'

'But we can't stay on land very long,' Pat said. 'It isn't good for our fur.'

'Oh, they'll soon go away. They're cross at the moment because they didn't catch us but they'll move off and then we can go back to the kelp patch.'

Soon the sharks gave up and went away. Pat and Bobby looked at each other. Their fur had dried and stood up in little tufts all over them.

'You were right, Pat,' said Bobby. 'It isn't good for our fur if we stay on land. We must get really wet before we try to swim back to the kelp patch.'

So they played in the waves on the edge of the sea for a while. They were gentle waves, not like the rough ones of the day before.

Pat pushed Bobby off a rock, and slid in after him. They splashed about, rolling one another over and over until their coats were sleek and shiny again.

'Am I wet enough?' asked Pat.

'Yes,' said Bobby, 'but there's a bit of seaweed sticking to your fur. That's not good for you. Pull it off.'

So Pat did. 'You've got a bit of seaweed on you too,' she said. 'Round the back.'

Bobby scraped it off on a rock.

'Have I got it all off?' he said.

'No,' Pat said, and came over and pulled a little piece of weed off him.

'Now,' he said, 'I'm going to make sure you're waterproof.'

He pushed her underneath the waves. She floated to the surface perfectly well.

'You're all right. Now you do the same to me,' Bobby said. So Pat pounced on him. She pushed him under the water, and every time he came up she pushed him under again.

'That's enough,' spluttered Bobby. 'How can I breathe if you keep pushing me under?'

'Let's see if you can float properly,' said Pat.

Bobby lay on the water, and the air in his fur made him float perfectly.

'Isn't it dinner-time?' asked Pat. 'I'm hungry.'

'Yes, we've been out for hours,' said Bobby. 'At least we weren't eaten by those sharks.'

They darted swiftly through the water, back to the kelp patch.

Pat's mother was worried and angry.

'Where have you been?' she asked.

'You're supposed to tell me when you are going away for a long time.'

'We didn't know,' said Pat. 'We were chased by sharks. But I knew just what to do.'

Her mother wasn't taken in by her boasting.

'Oh, my goodness,' she said, 'I'm so glad you had Bobby with you.'

'Now listen, you two,' Carrie said. 'You must be hungry after that adventure. Go away and find something to eat, and don't come back till bed-time.'

'Why?' asked Pat.

'You'll see why then,' said Carrie. 'It's a surprise.'

So Pat and Bobby went diving with some of the other sea otters, and Pat got an armful of sea urchins. She was just coming up to breathe and to eat them when her whole catch was snatched from underneath her. She called Bobby.

'Oh, I know who that was,' he said. 'We call her Snatcher. She's too lazy to dive if she can steal from someone smaller than herself. She had better not try it again, though. Here, have some of mine.'

'I thought all sea otters helped each other,' Pat sniffed, while she munched.

'No, there are bad sea otters, I'm afraid,' said Bobby, 'just as there are some dangerous fish like sharks and some bad men who hunt otters. You know about them, I suppose?'

'No,' said Pat doubtfully. She seemed to be learning about all the nasty things today.

'Well, it doesn't happen much now. But once men used to chase us with clubs to take our fur to help keep them warm.'

'Why are they cold?' asked Pat.

'Men are all bare, without fur, poor things,' said Bobby. 'And fishermen don't like us going near the lovely big shellfish called abalone. Sometimes they will shoot us if we do. But some good men look after sick otters, and help us to find new homes.'

'Why do we want new homes?' asked Pat. 'Tell me. I want to know *everything*.'

'We'd better go back to your mother. It's nearly bed-time.'

They soon found out about the surprise. Pat's mother was fast asleep with a baby lying on her – all wrapped up in the kelp. The baby was covered in fur and had its eyes open.

'Don't wake your mother,' Carrie said. 'You can talk in the morning. It's a little brother for you, Pat.'

It had been a very exciting day – too exciting in fact – but it had had a happy ending. For once, Pat did not ask any questions. She went straight to sleep with her paws over her eyes and a smile on her face.

Pat meets the Gaffer

The next morning, after Pat and Bobby had had breakfast and talked to Pat's mother for a while, Carrie called them over.

'Would you baby-sit while I go diving?' she said. 'As it's calm I think Pat could hold the baby this time.'

Bobby's sister was a big pup and Pat was quite small, so Carrie was very careful when she put the pup on to her chest.

'You look after them,' she winked at Bobby. He knew what she meant.

Then the mothers swam off. Pat was soon complaining.

'She's very heavy, and she wriggles like an octopus.'

'Shall I take her then?' asked Bobby.

'No, she's lovely really,' Pat said. 'But I mustn't forget and eat her, must I, as if she *were* an octopus?'

'No, of course you mustn't,' said Bobby, horrified. 'Just hold her carefully. Sing to her or something.'

Pat began mewing gently: 'Meeow, meeow.'

The pup had never heard such a peculiar noise before. She started, rolled over, and fell into the water. Fortunately she could float. Bobby laughed and laughed, and then picked her up and put her back on Pat.

'I like this,' said Pat. 'I feel important, holding the baby.'

'I know what you mean,' said Bobby. 'I feel the same when I have to look after silly little otters who ask too many questions!'

Pat stuck her tongue out at him – she couldn't do anything else when holding the pup.

'I know what we can do for her,' Bobby said. 'Think of a name. She hasn't got one yet.'

'I know,' Pat said. 'Yeller. Just listen to her.'

'She just wants some milk,' said Bobby. 'But I've thought of a good name. We like molluscs, so we'll call her Molly.'

'I like Molly,' said Pat. 'But what's a mollusc?'

'It's the proper name for a shellfish,' Bobby said. 'Gaffer told me.'

When Carrie came back she found the pup had a name. She was pleased. After that Pat went to see if they could hold her baby brother.

'No, he's too small for that, but you can watch over him when I've gone,' said her mother.

Baby brother was asleep, and his mother slipped quietly from under him, leaving him floating, still wrapped in the kelp. When she came back she slipped under him again, and he never knew she had been away.

Then Bobby decided that he had better go and join the male otters, particularly as Gaffer was supposed to be giving a special talk.

'Will they let me listen, too?' asked Pat.

'We'll ask,' said Bobby.

When they arrived at the males' kelp patch, Dud, a young otter, came over to meet them.

'Where's Gaffer?' asked Bobby. 'I want him to meet Pat.'

'He'll be here soon. He's giving us a talk in a few minutes.'

'I know. Pat wants to know everything and I can't tell her any more. Can you ask Gaffer if she can listen?'

Dud went away and came back in a few minutes. 'You can see him now. Come on.'

Pat liked Gaffer at first sight, and Gaffer liked her. 'But you know,' he said, 'we don't usually have females with us.'

'But I'm not just a female,' said Pat. 'I'm an otter who wants to know.'

'And she asks us too many questions we can't answer,' said Bobby. 'Please let her stay.'

'Well, of course she can stay,' laughed Gaffer. 'But stay at the back.'

Gaffer began his talk. 'Today I have something important to say. But first I must say something about the past, the history of the Sea Otter.'

Pat was impatient to ask her first question. 'Please, Gaffer, why are we called Sea Otters? We don't call men "Land Men".'

'We're not the only kind of otter,' Gaffer said. 'There are some skinny things, a quarter our size, called Land Otters who live on land and in rivers. But they are not much like us really. They don't even eat octopus.'

A gasp of horror came from the young otters. 'What do they eat then?' someone asked.

'Mostly fish, I think,' said Gaffer. 'Now, where were we? Oh yes. We used to live all round the shores of this great sea, the Pacific, but now there are only a few groups here and there. This was the fault of the men at first, when they hunted us for fur.'

'I told you so,' whispered Bobby.

'Shssh,' hissed the other otters.

'Now they aren't allowed to kill us, but they catch some of our best food,' Gaffer went on.

'But that's not fair,' said Dud. 'We're so short of food already.'

'Yes,' said Gaffer. 'The real trouble is that there are too many of us. Some of us are going

to have to move to where there is more food. This isn't the right time of the year because of the gales. But when spring comes we'll move along the coast to where our ancestors – that's the otters before us – used to live. It's colder there, and there shouldn't be many men about. There'll be plenty of food for us all.'

'Spring's a long time off,' grumbled one otter. 'I'm always hungry now.'

'Yes,' replied Gaffer, 'so until we can move we're going to have to hunt farther for food. Go out to sea more, and have fish and squid instead of shellfish. By the way, did you know that at one time we used to be known as the Old Man of the Sea because of our whiskers?'

'How do you know?' Pat asked very bravely.

'Oh, my father told me and his father told him and so on. We old-timers know lots of things because other old-timers told us them.'

'Am I an Old Man of the Sea?' asked Pat.

'Well, you have very fine whiskers,' Gaffer said, and everybody laughed. 'Now, that's the end of my talk. It's your turn now. I want all you Young Men of the Sea to go and tell your mothers and friends what I have said, so that they know that in the spring we shall have to move from here.'

The otters all jumped up and down which was the only way they could clap, and so show they were pleased. Then Bobby and Pat went back to their kelp patch. After they had had some food and a wash, they told their mothers what Gaffer had said.

'He's right,' said Carrie. 'It's getting harder to find food, and it's a good idea to move in the spring.'

'It will be difficult to find a place where there aren't any men. They seem to be everywhere,' said Bobby.

'There are wilder places, away from the cities,' Pat's mother said. 'Gaffer will know them.'

'I like Gaffer,' said Pat. 'There are so many things I'd like to ask him.'

'That'll give *me* a rest,' said her mother.

'Gaffer knows everything,' said Bobby. 'And he said that we could go and talk to him at any time, if we wanted to.'

'Oh, lovely!' said Pat. 'I shall ask him lots of questions. I shall ask him . . .'

And she went to sleep thinking of all the things she wanted to know.

Rescue by Man

Next morning Bobby woke Pat up with a sea urchin. 'It's not really your breakfast,' he said; 'it's very small, but there don't seem to be any bigger ones.'

'Never mind,' Pat said. 'I'll come with you and we'll find some more in a minute.'

They went as far as their little inlet where there was more food, but this time Snatcher followed them. Bobby stayed by Pat because he thought that Snatcher would not miss the chance to steal from a good little hunter like Pat. So when Pat yelled 'She's taken it!' Bobby chased Snatcher. He was as big as she was, and he gave her a good *bonk* on the nose and got the food back. He took it to Pat and then, when Snatcher rose to the surface for air, she found Bobby waiting for her.

'Go and do your own hunting, you lazy lump,' he said. 'And if you must steal, choose someone your own size. Keep away from Pat in future.'

Snatcher dived deep underwater, and Bobby went back to Pat.

'I don't think you'll have any more trouble with her,' he said.

'Good,' said Pat. 'But look, it wasn't only Snatcher who followed us.'

Bobby looked round. Lots of other otters had found their special place.

'We'll have to find another place of our own,' said Bobby. 'Never mind. Come on, we'll go back to the kelp patch.'

When they got back it was to see that Molly was lying in the water with her head resting on her mother.

'She's learning to swim,' Aunt Carrie said. She moved gently away, leaving the pup floating on the water.

Pat's new baby brother was fast asleep on *his* mother.

'I've had my breakfast,' she said. 'Aunt Carrie fetched some sea urchins for me.' She turned to Bobby. 'Your sister's growing up. She will be able to go hunting with you soon.'

But she never did, because over the next

few weeks it got harder and harder to find any food. Bobby and Pat began to feel hungrier and hungrier and to look thin and scraggy. Their mothers were busy trying to find enough food for the new pups, so they were left very much to themselves. Every day they had a long talk with Gaffer. There was so much to learn, and it helped them to forget how hungry they were. Pat asked him one question after another.

One day there was a storm. Pat and Bobby were some distance from the kelp patch when they were washed up on a beach by a big wave. The tide went out and there they were lying on the sand.

'Never mind,' Bobby said. 'When the tide comes in we'll get out to sea again.'

Pat dozed off for a while. Then she heard

a crunching noise on the beach.

It got nearer and nearer and then
stopped.

She looked up and yelped. Two strange
creatures were looking down at her. She knew
they must be men. One had white hair.

'It's all right,' said Bobby. 'I don't think
they mean any harm. They haven't got any
clubs with them, only nets on sticks.'

The men made odd noises to each other. Pat guessed they were talking. 'I wonder why they can't talk properly like us?' she thought.

And then, suddenly, the nets were pushed underneath them. Before Pat and Bobby knew what was happening they were each in a net, being carried up the beach over the men's shoulders.

Pat was frightened. 'What's happening? Where are they taking us?' she called, but Bobby couldn't hear her.

He was furious. He forgot how exhausted and hungry he was and chewed the net fiercely. But the nets didn't crack like shellfish, and soon he gave up.

The men took them a long way up the beach to some low buildings. Pat and Bobby had never seen anything like them before.

They felt very cold and miserable.

Then they had a surprise. They were taken into a warm room, and slipped from the nets into a bath of warm water. It was lovely.

The younger man gave Bobby a fish. He immediately held it for Pat to eat: she was too weak to hold it herself. The man laughed and called his friend to watch. Then they gave Bobby a fish for himself. That went down very quickly, and the men found themselves being stared at hopefully by two pairs of sad, round eyes. The message was very clear and they were given two more fish each.

When the meal was finished the sea otters had just enough energy left to clean themselves. Then the man with white hair picked Pat out of the water. Bobby tried to stop him, but he was too late. But it was all right. The man

quickly wrapped her in a towel and dried
her gently and put her on a warm mattress.
When he saw this, Bobby let the younger
man do the same to him. He turned to Pat.

'Feeling better?' he asked.

'Yes,' she said. 'Gaffer was right,
wasn't he?'

'That there are good men and bad men?'
Bobby said. 'Yes, these must be good men.
I wonder how they know so much about otters?'
he went on. 'They knew we needed to be
warm, and that they mustn't touch our fur
with their bare hands, in case it makes us sink.'

Suddenly he was worried. Pat hadn't
asked a single question for at least two
minutes. That wasn't like her. He need not
have worried: she was fast asleep, and soon
he was too.

When they awoke they were fed again and sponged down to make sure their fur was clean. At bed-time they were bathed again.

Next morning Pat and Bobby were given more fish, and they called for more when the men thought they had had enough. It was a very loud noise. The men were delighted and laughed. Then they talked to each other, and one opened the door of the hut.

Bobby sniffed. 'I know that smell,' he said. 'Come on, Pat.'

'Is it the sea?' asked Pat.

They followed the men outside, where there was a large pool full of salt water. In a moment they were in the water, lying on their backs.

When evening came, the men looked to see if they needed to be brought indoors again. But there they were, on their backs with their paws over their eyes, well-fed and happy – and fast asleep.

In the swim

Bobby and Pat woke up early next morning.

'I'm hungry,' Pat said. 'When can we eat?'

'We'll just have to wait,' Bobby said.
'Men don't get up as early as we do!'

'Oh,' said Pat, 'what's that up there?
Some kind of bird?'

Bobby laughed, 'I see you are wanting
to know again. Gaffer told me about those.
That's an aeroplane.'

'A what?'

'An aeroplane. It's a bird that man makes to carry things and people in. It has an engine in it. Listen!'

Pat listened to the aeroplane. Of course Bobby was right. 'It doesn't move its wings,' she said.

'No, and it doesn't sing like a bird,' said Bobby, teasing her, 'and it doesn't lay eggs either. The engine pulls it along.'

'Oh,' said Pat doubtfully. She didn't understand at all, but didn't like to say so.

By now the white-haired man was at the edge of the pool with a basket. But instead of throwing the fish, he held one up in his hand. Bobby jumped out of the water and grabbed it. Then Pat tried to do the same and nearly bit the man's hand off. Both Pat and the man looked very worried, but then Bobby and the men laughed.

The two men talked for a minute, and the younger one went away. When he came back he was wearing just swimming trunks. He came and stood on the edge of the pool, shivering.

Pat was sorry for him. 'He's all bare,' she said, 'except for that coloured thing round his middle. He looks frozen.'

'I told you that men don't have fur like us,' said Bobby. 'You'd think he would sink if he came into the water.'

At that moment the young man dived in. He was a good swimmer and swam overarm as fast as he could to the other end of the pool, turned under the water, and swam back.

Bobby wasn't at all impressed. 'Fancy waving his arms about and all that splashing with his legs. I'm sure he'd go faster if he didn't waste his energy like that.'

'Why hasn't he got webbed feet like us?' asked Pat. 'They would help him.'

The man changed to breast stroke.

'That's better,' said Pat. 'But doesn't he look silly when his head comes out of the water – just like a fish, with his mouth open like that. In fact, I'll call him Fishface.'

'Look at the way he kicks his feet,' said Bobby. 'It *must* be because they aren't webbed. And he hasn't got a big tail to steer him. Man does have a silly shape.'

Just then Fishface turned over on his back and floated beside them.

'That's nice,' said Pat, 'I am glad he doesn't sink. Do you know what?'

'No,' said Bobby. 'I don't want to, either.'

'Oh,' said Pat, 'B . . . b . . . boy otters! I was going to say that I think Fishface would like a game. Let's see!'

She paddled round him, and then pulled him under the water. They tussled a bit, and then Bobby nudged them to the surface again.

'Careful,' he said. 'Men can't stay under water as long as we can. You'll drown him.'

Certainly the man looked very red in the face. Pat quickly swam towards him to make sure he was all right, but Fishface thought she was going to play again.

'Aa-rr-wac,' he yelled. 'Aa-rr-wac.'

Pat was startled. Bobby laughed. 'Perhaps Fishface isn't quite so silly as we thought, if he knows our words for "Stop! Help!" Let's see if we can persuade him to say anything more.'

But the man didn't seem to know any more sea otter words. Soon man and otters all lay quietly on their backs together. The man even held Pat's front paw for a while. She liked that.

The older man was looking on. He took a mussel and a stone from a basket, and threw them to Fishface.

'I bet he doesn't know what to do with them,' Pat said. But the man did. He placed the stone on his chest, and rapped the mussel on it. He wasn't a very good shot, and he hit himself a good deal before the mussel broke. Then he handed it to Pat, and climbed out of the water.

Bobby made it quite clear that he wasn't going to be left out. 'What about me?' he called. It needed more than one mussel from the man to make him be quiet.

Later they saw Fishface go off with one of the nets. When he came back he had another otter in it. Pat stood up, her eyes bright, her whiskers quivering. 'Who is it?' she asked. 'Is it someone we know? Do you think it's Gaffer?'

She and Bobby watched the man go into the warm hut.

'I am going to see who it is,' Bobby said. 'You stay here while I find out.' But of course Pat followed him to the hut.

They banged on the door with their paws, and Whitehair (that's what they called him) opened it, with a look of surprise on his face. They just lolloped past him, straight to the bath.

It wasn't Gaffer. It was Dud, the young otter, looking very ill indeed. He was even refusing the fish he had been offered. He had never been known to refuse food in his life.

'Come on, Dud,' said Bobby. 'Eat up. They're nice men, and they'll soon have you well.'

'You're sure they're not just fattening us for our coats?' asked Dud.

'No, I don't think so. Pat is certainly getting fatter, but they don't seem to want her coat – though Fishface could do with it!'

Dud needed no more encouragement. He ate up the fish, and was soon dried and lying on the mattress. Pat and Bobby lay beside him, until he fell asleep. Then they noticed the men throwing some mussels into the pool, so they quickly went there for their supper.

As they lay on their backs before going to sleep, Pat turned to Bobby.

'Do you know, I feel different,' she said. 'I've been too interested all day to ask many questions. What do you think that means?'

'It means that you are almost fit to live with,' said Bobby. 'Or you would be, if you let me go to sleep. Goodnight.'

Together again

The next morning Pat and Bobby went in to see how Dud was. He was better but puzzled. 'I don't understand it,' he said. 'I am still hungry, but I can't eat any more. It's not fair!'

'I'll finish it,' said Pat, who always managed to eat everything she was given.

'Stop it, you pig,' said Bobby. 'Dud can't eat because he has been hungry for so long. If *you* eat his food the men will think he is better than he really is!'

Pat was just starting to argue, when the men came in and shooed them out. Shortly afterwards the men went off again with the nets.

At the bottom of the pool Pat found the stone they had used to break the mussels. She picked it up and banged the side of the pool with it. A small piece of cement broke off. She was surprised. She kept banging away until she had made quite a big hole.

It was some time before Bobby noticed what she was doing. 'Don't do that!' he said. 'If you make the hole bigger, the water will run away!'

She didn't believe him, but just at that moment the men came back. Fishface was staggering under something big and heavy.

Whitehair stood by roaring with laughter and then they went into the hut.

Bobby looked at Pat. 'I think that is another sea otter,' he said. 'A big one.'

'Is it Gaffer?' asked Pat. 'Oh, I hope it's Gaffer!'

They jumped out of the pool and waddled through the open door of the hut. Looking at them from a half-empty bath was Gaffer. Beside him, drenched to the skin, was Fishface, his mouth wide open with astonishment. Gaffer had not waited to be lifted in – he had jumped into the water, and most of it had splashed over the man!

Bobby and Pat mewed delightedly, and Pat jumped into the bath with Gaffer because she was so pleased to see him. What little water was left in the bath went over Whitehair this time. He wasn't amused.

'Oh, Gaffer,' Pat squeaked, 'we thought you were dead.'

'Get off my stomach, young otter,' said
Gaffer, 'and tell me what's going on here.'

So they told him all about themselves
and Dud. When he was offered some fish he
lumbered out of the bath and persuaded
Dud to eat it.

'What happens next?' Gaffer asked Bobby.

'One of them puts you on his lap and
dries you with a towel,' chuckled Bobby. 'I
wonder if his lap is strong enough?'

Gaffer glared at him, and waddled up to
Whitehair, who dried him on the ground. Then
all the otters got on the mattress together.

'These men may mean well,' said Gaffer,
'but they are not very clever. I watched them
for a time picking shellfish off the rocks, and
they were so slow. A few swipes with a good
stone and I had doubled their store, weak

as I am. I guessed they had come to take us where food was more plentiful, but I had to climb into the net myself, while they were still discussing how to get me into it. They were very surprised.'

'What do you think they are going to do with us?' quavered Dud, who was still very weak and frightened.

'I don't know,' said Gaffer. 'But they wouldn't take all this trouble if they were only going to kill us for our fur. You have a rest, Dud, and Bobby and Pat can take me outside and show me this pool they talk about.'

Outside, they found the men staring glumly at the hole in the side of the pool. Pat slid into the water as if she knew nothing about the hole!

The men began sawing up lengths of wood. Gaffer went over to see what they were doing. They looked nervously at him as he stood near, his bright eyes watching. He looked as if he might tell them they were doing it all wrong.

'What are they making?' asked Pat later, when the otters were in the pool together.

'I think they are building cages,' said Gaffer. 'They must be going to take us somewhere else quite soon.'

'One cage is much larger than the others. But do you think it's strong enough for you, Gaffer?' Pat asked.

'That's enough cheek from you, young otter,' he replied. 'I'm going back to the hut now to keep Dud company for the night. Goodnight, both of you. It's good to see you again, even if you have forgotten your manners. Sleep well!'

Journey by air

The next few days were very exciting for the otters – there was so much to see. The men were busy finishing the cages.

Dud was so much better now that he had enough to eat that he was allowed in the pool. The four otters played there together, twisting, turning and darting in the water. When they were fed it was very noisy. The otters went *bang, bang, bang* with their shellfish on their pebbles. Sometimes, when no one was looking, the young ones banged on the side of the pool. The men went *bang, bang, bang* with their hammers on the cages.

One day a big lorry arrived. The two men brought the cages to the edge of the pool. Bobby and Pat and Dud didn't like the look of them at all. But Gaffer was excited.

'Come on,' he said. 'They're ready for us.' And he climbed out of the pool. The others followed him.

Whitehair looked at Gaffer in surprise and then opened the door of the big cage. He hadn't expected it to be so easy. Gaffer waddled straight in, and the door was closed behind him. In a minute or two Bobby, Pat and Dud were in their cages. Then the cages were lifted into the lorry. Whitehair took a last look at the sea otters as if he were sorry to see them go. Fishface put a large box of food in the back, some cans of water, and a watering can. Then he climbed in with the driver, and off they went.

The journey didn't last long. The lorry was unloaded. Suddenly a loud noise split the air – quite the loudest noise Pat had ever heard. 'What is it? What is it?' she cried, very frightened.

Bobby was scared too, but he soon recovered. 'It's all right,' he said. 'It's one of those man-made birds you saw the other day. You can see it if you look out of your cage.'

Gaffer spoke up. 'I think we're going for a ride in it,' he said. 'Won't that be exciting? You mustn't be afraid of new things, you know.'

Of course Gaffer was right. A little later

they were being carried up the gangway to
the aeroplane's door. A man in uniform took
one end of each cage and Fishface the other.

Gaffer's cage caused
more trouble than
all the others put
together. The door
of the plane was
only just wide
enough to take it. Gaffer
glared at the man in uniform
every time they got stuck. The poor man
became quite nervous and was glad when
Gaffer was finally in position.

There were a lot of people waiting to get
on the plane and they all watched closely.
When it was Pat's turn to go on she was
frightened again. Fishface took her paw for
a minute and said something. She didn't
understand, but she was comforted.

The cages of the three younger otters

were put in a row with Gaffer beside them so that they could all talk to him. As the passengers passed them on the way to their seats they stared at the cages, and Gaffer stared back. He was just as interested in them as they were in him!

The plane was kept cool for the sea otters. It was far too cool for the passengers' liking. But they had been warned and had brought warm clothes to put on. Soon the pilot came on board, seat belts were fastened and the engines started.

When they began to move Pat was frightened again. She reached out through the bars and grabbed Fishface's trousers. He looked down and smiled to comfort her. Bobby in the next cage to Pat said, 'Oh, this is exciting. We're going up and up and up into the sky.'

'I wish my tummy would come with me,' Gaffer said. 'It feels as though I've left it behind. Perhaps that is why the humans all wear seat belts – to keep their tummies in.'

Finally the plane levelled out. 'That's nice,' said Dud. 'It's not nearly as bumpy as the sea when the waves are rough.'

It wasn't. Pat almost began to enjoy it. Gaffer had been right. It was exciting. Then she started to ask questions again. Where were they going? How long would the journey take? And when would they have something to eat?

The passengers were asking Fishface questions too. Fishface had to tell them all about the otters. Gaffer looked at him as he answered as if he would like to answer for him. After all, he knew more about otters than Fishface did!

'I'm getting hungry,' said Pat to Bobby. 'Shouldn't we remind Fishface?'

'No,' said Dud. 'When he's finished talking he'll feed us. I can smell he's got something delicious in that box by his side.'

Fishface must have guessed. He pushed some mussels through the bars for each of them. A little girl came over to help. She was given fish to give the otters, but had to be stopped from trying to stroke them. Then she gave them each a pebble, and stared while they cracked the mussels. In the confined space of the plane the noise of bashing was shattering.

Everyone in the plane was listening and

laughing. They had been brought coffee and biscuits, so they were eating too.

After a while it got warmer and their man filled a watering can and sprinkled it on the cages. The little girl tried to help but only succeeded in watering her own shoes. Her parents were not pleased at all.

Later on the otters began to feel hungry again. They wanted their lunch and they began calling for it. The man had to explain what all the noise was about, so the people joined in too.

'Meeow, meeow, meeow,' they called. The hostess came rushing in, and laughed when she was told the reason.

The otters were fed straight away and then the passengers were too. Then the lights near their cages were switched off, and they were able to go to sleep.

Return to the sea

The otters all woke up when the plane landed. Pat was frightened at first, and then remembered what Gaffer had said. It was new and exciting, but nothing to be afraid of. Gaffer watched her, and was pleased.

When they landed, the passengers waited to say goodbye. It had been cold, but quite the most interesting journey they had ever had, so they all joined in a loud 'meeow' as the cages were put into a lorry. Other people at the airport thought they were mad.

The lorry stopped beside a ship. They could smell the sea, and hear the water lapping against its side. There were many other cages there, and Pat was put next to a young girl sea otter who was frightened. Pat comforted her, and explained what Gaffer had told her.

'Oh, thank you,' said the young otter. 'You are clever. How do you know so much?'

The ship set off, and soon they came to an island where the cages were landed and opened. Gaffer came out slowly from his cage and looked around. All he could see was one small hut and lots of birds. A little way out to sea was a kelp patch. It looked an ideal place for sea otters.

Suddenly a group of young otters started to rush past him. Gaffer coughed, and looked hard at them. They stopped immediately, and waited till all the otters were released.

'Now,' Gaffer said, 'we must all keep together until we have looked around. I expect some more grown-up otters will join us soon, but until then Bobby will lead the boys and Pat will look after the girls. They know what to do.'

Pat was horrified. She had never looked after anybody in her life. Other people had looked after her. She just asked questions.

Bobby saw the look on her face, and laughed. 'Don't be worried,' he said. 'Gaffer and I will still look after you. But you *do* know what to do, don't you? Isn't that why you asked questions?'

So they all swam out to a nearby kelp patch. They spent ages playing in the kelp and diving for food. Dud ate far too much, and felt quite ill.

'Serve you right,' said Pat. 'You're just greedy.'

Dud stared at her. 'Me, greedy?' he said. 'You're a fine one to talk. Why, only yesterday . . .'

Pat interrupted him. 'Yesterday was yesterday,' she said airily. 'I didn't know much then!'

That night they were very tired, and Pat was very quiet. 'Something wrong?' said Bobby. 'You haven't asked a question for ages. Don't you want to know anything more? You don't know everything, you know.'

'No,' said Pat, 'I was wondering about our mothers and the babies. Will we ever see them again? I miss them a lot.'

Gaffer overheard. 'We will have to wait and see,' he said. 'But I don't think they would only bring youngsters, so keep hoping. Goodnight.'

The next morning they saw the ship coming back with more cages. Some of the cages were very big, larger than Gaffer's. As the cages opened, a number of mothers and babies came out.

The young otters were all watching. Suddenly Pat saw her mother and then Carrie – both with their babies. An excited mewing filled the air as the new arrivals took to the water.

They all went out to the kelp patch, and talked and played together.

Suddenly Gaffer called out, 'Look, there goes the boat.'

It had left the island and was circling the kelp patch. Fishface was standing at one side.

'He's going,' called Pat. 'Let's say goodbye.'

So they circled round the boat, calling and splashing. And Pat jumped right out of the water, nudging Fishface's outstretched hand. He looked both happy and sad. Then the boat turned and slowly disappeared.

That night Pat slept close to her mother and her little brother. They talked about all their adventures, and the way that Fishface had looked after them. And Pat told her mother she had been in charge of the girl otters for a whole night.

'I am glad that I wanted to know,' she said. 'I couldn't have done that otherwise.'

Then she put her paws over her eyes and went to sleep.

This is Plop.

Plop is a baby barn owl.

He is fat and fluffy.

He has big, round eyes.

He has soft, downy feathers.

He is perfect in every way,

except for just ONE thing . . .

Read another Jill Tomlinson
and find out more.

This is Suzy.

Suzy is a small stripy cat.

Suzy likes: living in France, chasing butterflies and being stroked the wrong way.

Suzy doesn't like: getting lost . . .

Read another Jill Tomlinson and find out more.

This is Hilda.

Hilda is a small, speckled hen.

Hilda likes cornflakes, fire-engines and visiting her auntie.

But there is one thing that Hilda would like more than anything else . . .

Read another Jill Tomlinson and find out more.